THE FOUR DEATHS AND ONE RESURRECTION OF FYODOR MIKHAILOVICH

Zoran Živković

The Four Deaths and One Resurrection
of Fyodor Mikhailovich

Quotations from Dostoevsky's works, written in italic, are from the translations by Richard Pevear and Larissa Volokhonsky. Used with permission.

ISBN: 978-4-908793-58-5

Cover: Youchan Ito, Togoru Art Works

Neoclassic Fleurons font used with permission of
Paulo W–Intellecta Design

Cadmus Press
cadmusmedia.org

THE FOUR DEATHS AND ONE RESURRECTION OF FYODOR MIKHAILOVICH

Zoran Živković

Translated from the Serbian
by
Randall A. Major

Cadmus Press
2024

Dedicated to Zoran and Slobodan, to whom,
on Saturday evenings,
I read this book while it was being written...

Contents

1. The Park

"FYODOR MIKHAILOVICH! FYODOR MIKHAILOVICH!"

A male voice followed me as I reached the lamp post. It was just a flicker of light amidst the turbid darkness all around me.

The morning had not foretold such a storm. It was brisk but sunny, with just a few clouds in the clear autumn sky. Then in the early afternoon, heavy clouds had begun to gather. By dusk, the storm had ensued: it was simultaneously raining and snowing, and a fog had settled in. Before long, it had turned into a real blizzard.

The wind howled in the deserted streets, heaving the black water of the Fontanka higher than the mooring rings and perkily brushing up against the skinny streetlamps of the embankment, which in their turn seconded its howling with a thin, shrill creaking, which made up an endless, squeaking, rattling concert, quite familiar to every inhabitant of Petersburg.

Streams of rainwater, broken up by the wind, sprayed almost horizontally. Amid the night's silence, broken only by the distant rumble of carriages, the howling of the wind, and the creaking of the streetlamps, the splashing and burbling water pouring down from all the roofs, porches, gutters, and eaves onto the granite pavement of the sidewalks had a dismal sound.

There was not a soul either near or far, nor did it seem

there could be. I myself would not have even dreamed of sticking my nose out if I hadn't had an unpostponable meeting with a friend in Shestilavochnaya Street. Perhaps I would find him no longer alive tomorrow. I stood for a while in front of the building's entrance in the vague hope that a carriage might come by and then, having no other choice, I set off on foot.

Holding my umbrella like a shield, more in front of me than overhead, I splashed my way slowly through the streets and alleyways. I was going through a familiar part of town, staying close to the façades of houses and buildings so that I did not even need to look ahead. However, after about half an hour, when I emerged in a large open area, I realized that it would have been better after all if I had looked up from time to time, even through the watery curtain that the wind would have thrown in my face. I had ended up outside a park that was not supposed to be there. I had obviously made a really bad turn.

It didn't seem alluring in the slightest to step into the sludge of snow, rain and fog before me, but any other choice would lead to a circuitous detour. I lowered the umbrella even further and set forth. I was engulfed immediately by the cloud. My route till now had had at least some light. Through the flocks of snow flurries peered the streetlights, porch lamps and occasional room windows. In the park, however, I could not even see my hand in front of my face.

I pushed onward with utmost care, trying to go straight down the wide path. After a few dozen steps, at a certain distance in front of me, I began to see a point of light now and then. At first I thought I was just imagining it, but as I approached it, the tiny light became ever clearer and larger, until I could finally see that it must be some sort of light fixture.

A lamp post stood at the intersection of two paths which crossed at right-angles. It formed a rather small circle of light on the ground, like a tiny island in the middle of a murky sea. The cone-shaped beam of the gaslight was dappled with large, twisting snowflakes which seemed to have no end.

The moment I stepped into the circle, someone suddenly called out to me. I flinched and quickly turned in the direction I thought the voice came from, but I saw no one, of course. As if an opaque wall rose outside the perimeter of the light.

From behind the wall, however, someone stepped out. It was a rather short, older man, with a hat pulled down over his forehead and wearing a long, heavy overcoat. He had tiny eyes behind his small, round, wire-framed glasses. He was huffing, as if he had been running.

"Fyodor Mikhailovich!" he repeated in excitement, and then approached me. It took him a while to catch his breath. "Oh, it's really good I found you!"

"And who are you?"

He ignored my question. "Did you see him?"

"Who?"

"So, you didn't. This damned blizzard, it's making my life miserable. Listen, you must not leave here. For any reason! It is of utmost importance. There is a big disturbance. Really big! I'm off to continue pursuit. While there's still time."

"I don't understand a thing you're saying. Who are you looking for? How do you know who I am? And who are you?"

"I don't have time to explain right now. It's just important that you stay here. If he shows up, you must detain him. Whatever it takes. You will recognize him."

He turned and vanished into the flurries in two quick steps.

I remained standing there in confusion as the questions swarmed through my head. The primary one—who was this man?—was not hard to figure out. A policeman, of course. Would anyone else be wildly chasing someone through this weather in the darkness of the park, and evidently not himself be on the wrong side of the law? Yes, but what kind of policeman? Most likely not a beat cop. They send uniformed men on manhunts, certainly younger than this fellow who was at least a dozen years my senior. So it must be the Third Section. That meant this was all about something more serious than a banal robbery or something of the kind. The secret police are primarily interested in political transgressions.

I shuddered at the thought. If some sort of political crime was supposed to take place this very night in the park, then I was out of luck. Who would ever believe that I just happened to be here because I had got lost in the storm? And now it was too late for me to vanish discreetly because I had already been made. That's why the inspector hadn't wasted time on me. Someone else was his main target, and it was enough to tell me to wait for him here because he knew I had nowhere to run. They would easily find me wherever I hid.

There were a few unclear things in what he had so quickly said. What kind of big disturbance was at hand? The greatest disturbance would be a threat to his imperial majesty. Was he in great danger at this very moment, because otherwise what would it mean, "While there's still time"? And if that were true, why wasn't the park swarming with men from the Third Section, instead of one aging, huffing inspector chasing after the conspirators?

Actually, the thing worrying me most was that he was convinced I would recognize the principal for whom he was looking. How would I recognize him? I had no connections whatsoever with anarchists or revolutionaries who would dare attack the emperor. I didn't know any of them. Unless—again I shuddered—someone was in my social circle and I hadn't the faintest idea that he was an anarchist or revolutionary in secret. What kind of surprise awaited me when they caught him?

At that instant it seemed to me that a shadow slipped over the dark-grey wall in front of me, as if someone had moved a step or two back from the circle of light. It could easily have been an illusion caused by the heavy, windblown snow. Still, I looked carefully in front of me and pricked up my ears. Several long moments passed. Even if there were any sounds in my vicinity, they were all damped down by the howling wind. When someone did speak from the unseen beyond, such a shudder went through me that I thought in a panic I was certainly about to have an epileptic fit.

"Good evening," someone said in my voice.

"Good evening," I responded after a lengthy hesitation, when it became clear that I could not move. My legs were disobeying me, even though I so deeply wished to flee wildly from this lighted spot, anywhere into the safety of the storm's darkness.

"He'll be back soon to check if you've seen me. Tell him you haven't. Let him go on looking for me."

"You want me to lie to an agent of the Third Section?"

"He's not any sort of secret agent. And you wouldn't be lying. You still haven't seen me, have you?"

"No, but your voice..."

"Here he comes!" I was interrupted by my voice from the darkness.

For about half a minute I stood waiting in the middle of the white whirlwind, and then from the wall of the cone, right in front of me, only his head appeared, wearing his glasses and the hat that was now piling up with snow.

"Did you see him?"

Fearing that my voice might betray me, I shook my head several times, harder than I should have. Fortunately, that didn't seem dubious to him.

"Where is he, damn him? He's toying with me, even though he knows how serious this is. And dangerous. All right, I'm off to look for him again. At the cost of your life, don't move from here. If I lose you as well, everything is lost."

The head returned to the darkness.

Again about half a minute passed before my voice spoke out again nearby.

"He's quite comical, all panicky like this. I could barely keep myself from laughing."

"Nothing was funny to me. How can you toy with the poor guy if the situation is, as he says, so serious and dangerous?"

"This is your first time, isn't it?" he responded with a question.

"What?"

"That you find yourself in this—situation?"

"I don't know what kind of situation I've found myself in. Circumstances made me come out into this blizzard tonight. I got lost. I ended up in some kind of park and came across the two of you. From that moment on, everything has become a big, impossible, insane mess."

"Well, let's complete it then. I think you're ready now."

In the place where the head had just stuck out, into the lighted area emerged myself. That is, another me. That is, my perfect double. We were dressed the same: the same heavy winter overcoat, the same pants and galoshes, the same hat, the same black umbrella. Only the color of the long wool scarf was different: mine was dark blue, his was dark brown.

Even though my double's voice had somewhat prepared me for this confrontation, I still shuddered and stepped back slightly when I saw myself. Even a muffled "Ah!" escaped my lips.

"For me, the weather was bad the first time, too. Three and a half years ago. Not a blizzard but a really bad summer rainstorm. And it wasn't a park, but an unfamiliar square in town. I know exactly how you feel right now."

"I feel quite confused. I don't know what I should ask first..."

"I won't, unfortunately, have many answers, nor do we have much time."

"Who are you?"

"Fyodor Mikhailovich, a writer, just like you."

"But... but... that is not possible."

"That's exactly what I said back on the town square. And yet it is."

"Wait, this is just like my novelette—*The Double.* But *The Double* is fantastika. It can't be real. Am I perhaps just dreaming all this?"

"If you were dreaming, you would wake up after this question. That's the way it always is. Something else is happening. Reality is more fantastic than you can ever possibly imagine. Even more fantastic than in our *The Double.*"

"Our?"

"Yes, of course. I also wrote it."

Again I shook my head hard. "Nonsense! Two Fyodor Mikhailoviches who write the same things cannot exist. If they did, that would be the miracle of all miracles. And no one has ever heard of any such thing."

"They haven't, I agree. That is because there is only one Fyodor Mikhailovich in this world. But this is not the only world."

I squinted at my double. I saw that he was waiting for me to respond, but nothing reasonable crossed my mind.

"I was also left speechless," he went on when he realized that my response was not forthcoming. "Indeed, what can one say about such a crazy idea? Two worlds that overlap almost exactly. I'm from one, you're from the other, and we are as if we were identical twins. There are only a few minuscule differences between us."

"What kind of minuscule differences?" I finally spoke up.

"Well, like these." He first pointed at my scarf, then at his own. "Insignificant. They can also, however, be bigger, more important. When this happened to me the second time, fourteen months ago, there wasn't all the mayhem like now. I had more time to speak with my double. It turned out that our literary opus wasn't quite the same. I had written two novelettes he hadn't, and he a novel and three stories I hadn't..."

"Wait, wait," I interrupted him because something occurred to me right then. "Those two doubles you met—from three and a half years and from fourteen months ago—where did they come from? I am your only double, and the two of us are meeting for the first time just now."

My collocutor spent several moments just looking at me, and then he sighed.

"This will be the hardest part for you. At least it was for me. You are not my only double. Far from it. There are, actually, countless doubles, just as there are countless worlds from which they come."

"Countless how?" I inquired, also after a brief silence.

"I don't know. I don't understand that part in the least. Last time, when we met again, that old guy," he nodded over his shoulder at the invisibility behind him, "tried really hard to explain it to us both, but neither of us got it. The other worlds are called parallel, though it's not clear to me what that means. Even less intelligible to me is that those countless other worlds, it seems, are not even in our cosmos."

"Then where are they from? The cosmos is one. There are no others."

"It turns out that there are. But don't ask me how or why. About that, I'm completely in the dark."

"All right, no matter, parallel worlds, other cosmoses... Let's leave that aside. But how did you get here, to my world, from some other one, from some other cosmos?"

"Or you to mine?"

"I never left this one at all. As I told you, I set off to make an unpostponable visit. I got lost in the blizzard and found myself in this park, where I met you."

"It was exactly the same for me. My friend was on his deathbed, I had to go see him one last time. I was heading toward Shestilavochnaya Street. When I entered the park, I heard an old man call out my name. I recognized his voice and immediately realized what was happening. Angry at him because he had appeared again and would detain me, so I might not reach my dying friend in time, I decided to take my revenge on him by playing a little hide-and-seek."

"Why didn't you just keep going if you knew what was happening? By playing hide-and-seek, you are also wasting precious time. Both of us are, actually."

"Because it is impossible. As long as this keeps going, we cannot get out of the park. If you did try to get out, you would just keep going in circles, especially in this weather, like in a labyrinth with no exit. Only the old man knows where the gates are."

"Gates?"

"The passageways between worlds. Shortcuts. That's the answer to your question of how one gets from world to another."

"What do these gates look like?"

"They can't be seen at all. The old man tells you you're standing in front of one, you just take a few steps and pass right through it. Nothing happens, you don't feel anything, everything seems normal. You just find yourself on the other side, you are back in your world."

"But if this here is not my world, how did I get here? There was no old man to show me where the gate was."

"That's the key question. We are actually not supposed to be here. Access should not be at all possible. And yet, here we are."

"How does the old man explain that?"

"He doesn't. There are no explanations. He calls these spontaneous transfers 'disturbances'. It seems this evening's events are somehow special. He never said 'big disturbance' before."

"Who is that old man anyway?"

My double shrugged. "I have no idea. I tried to ask him, but he avoided answering me. He seems to be the one taking care that the disturbances, once they've happened, are removed as soon as possible. He's some sort of supervisor, guardian, or something like that. That's all I've ever figured out."

"Couldn't it have been someone a little more intelligent? This guy seems a bit confused to me."

"It just seems so to you. He's clever. It's my fault you got the wrong impression. I shouldn't be playing hide-and-seek with him."

"It would be good if he came right back, to put an end to this once and for all. My feet are already wet, and when I'm standing still like this, unmoving, it's very cold." I hesitated for a moment. "You must be cold, too."

"Indeed," he responded with a smile. "We are doubles in every sense of the word."

It seemed not quite in every sense, because the very next moment he looked inquisitively at the dark gray wall, as if he had heard something there, but nothing had reached my ears.

"Here he comes," he said quickly.

Through the perimeter of the cone, however, it wasn't just one figure who passed, as we expected, but two. Even though my double was markedly more experienced than me, this was new to him as well and he, like me, froze in surprise. With the old man arrived our—triple.

The first minute passed without a word being said as the three Fyodor Mihailoviches attentively measured each other up. The newcomer was also dressed entirely like us, only his scarf was crimson.

These observations would have continued had they not been interrupted by the old man who upbraided the dark brown scarf.

"It is truly unkind of you to toy with me like this. We are seeing each other for the third time now, and you know very well that these encounters are not some sort of joke. Especially not this evening. You are only my second set of triplets since I started doing this." He paused briefly. "All right, and now for the more important thing. There isn't much time till the gate closes. I hope," he turned toward me, "this joker informed you of what's basically going on." I nodded my head. "This gentleman," he nodded toward the crimson scarf, "needed no instructions, this is his second time." He was briefly silent again as he looked over the three identical faces. "Unfortunately, gentlemen, the news is not good. Triplets are always accompanied by a big disturbance. We cannot return you to the worlds from which you came here. Those gates are closed."

He waited a moment to see what kind of effect the news would have on us. We exchanged glances, but no one said anything.

"Three new ones have opened, and you are to choose who will go through which one. I can only give you two facts about what awaits you in your new world. The first gate leads to great longevity and little renown. Ninety years and the fewest books, not very good ones at that. The second leads to a medium life length and number of books. Seventy-five years and neither many nor few mediocre books. The third toward a short lifespan and great opus. Only sixty years, but a multitude of excellent books."

He turned to me again.

"Unfortunately, you are the only one who cannot choose. You'll have to take whatever is left over. The one who is meeting me for the third time now will choose first, followed by the one for whom it is the second meeting. I know it seems unfair, but those are the rules. Otherwise you would never come to an agreement."

He looked at the dark brown scarf inquisitively.

"Great longevity."

Then he turned to the crimson scarf, "So?"

"Everything medium."

"Satisfied?" the old man asked me finally.

We stood staring at each other for a while, until I shrugged my shoulders.

"What would you have chosen if you had had the chance?"

"You'll only find that out if we meet once again in fours. But the chances of that are not very high. I'm already fifty-nine..."

2. The Restaurant Car

The Inspector cleared his throat, but he said nothing immediately.

He looked slowly over the faces of the eight passengers in the restaurant car. Each was sitting at their own table, four on the left side, four on the right. There was another pair of tables at the entrance to the car. On the left was the Inspector, while on the right, across the aisle, there was no longer anyone.

Closest to the Inspector on the same side of the car, there was a girl who was probably thirteen or fourteen. *She was pale-haired and freckled.* She seemed to be *childish and quiet*, as if waiting for some sort of amusement.

Behind her sat a young man of quite inconspicuous appearance and outfit. You could be with him somewhere for quite a while, and later remember him as you would a piece of furniture. Yet, he was carefully watching the events around him, as if preparing to write about them later.

Third from the Inspector was a young woman of around twenty-two, *with a pale rosy tint on her broad face, and her lower lip protruding a bit, as if a little swollen. She had abundant dark red hair, dark sable eyebrows, and lovely gray blue eyes with long lashes.* Her beauty was not striking, but it did catch men's eyes.

Finally on the left side was a man in his mid-twenties, not remarkably handsome, but with regular, manly features. He had the spiritualized physiognomy of a person who is doubtless smart, perhaps even wise, but whose soul is harried by anxieties that he does not know how to contend with.

Across from him, on the right side, furthest from the Inspector, sat another beautiful girl in her early twenties. *Her hair, apparently dark blonde, was done simply, informally; her eyes were dark and deep, her forehead pensive; the expression of her face was passionate and as if haughty. Her face was somewhat thin, perhaps also pale.*

In front of her sat a man, *tall, about fifty-five years old or even a little more, with a purple-red, fleshy and flabby face framed by thick gray side-whiskers, with large, rather protruding eyes. His figure would have been rather imposing if there had not been something seedy, shabby, even soiled about it.*

At the middle table sat *a slender and trim woman, with dark brown hair.* From her gauntness and the *flushed spots on her cheeks*, it was evident that she was suffering from an illness, probably tuberculosis. She might have been thirty-something, though she looked at least a decade older because of her decaying health.

Finally, the last on the right side, closest to the Inspector, was *a tall, thin young man, black-haired and badly shaven* who had just turned twenty. Even though he was poorly dressed, he radiated a certain haughtiness and self-assuredness, as if saying that he would not allow life to break him.

"Ladies and gentlemen," the Inspector began at last, "I first owe you an apology for detaining you here a bit longer..."

"Almost an hour," he was interrupted by the reprimanding voice of the seedy gentleman to his right. "Unforgivable!"

"They didn't allow us to leave here," the tubercular lady hissed. "Not even to go to the toilet. And I need to go urgently, no matter what you say..." She began to get up.

The Inspector turned to the exit behind him and snapped his fingers. There immediately appeared a heavyset mustached policeman with a scar above his left eyebrow.

"Accompany this lady to the restroom."

"I don't need a chaperone!"

"Right this way, ma'am," grumbled the policeman, showing the way.

As she passed by the Inspector, the lady snorted, which made the young girl softly giggle.

"I tried to ask for a glass of water," said the red-haired beauty on the left. "To calm down a bit. All of this has shocked me. But they refused to serve me..."

"A waiter will soon come to take your orders," said the Inspector.

"So, you're going to keep us here longer?" the badly shaven young man asked.

"At least for a while. It's necessary."

"But why? What happened is clear. An accident. The poor man sitting there," he pointed at the table in front of him, "had a heart-attack. A tragic event, but not very unusual. There's nothing questionable in that..."

"Well then, please tell us what happened exactly. You were the closest, you could see it all best."

"I wasn't watching him... of course... all the time. There was no reason to. The gentleman was quietly eating, just like I was. I only looked up when he began to gurgle. He grabbed his chest, bugged out his eyes, opened his mouth as if trying to catch his breath or say something, then fell facedown into his plate."

The girl giggled again.

The Inspector shot her a reproving glance, then turned back to the young man.

"Grabbed himself by the chest?"

"Yes. That's the way it is with heart attacks. I've seen it before."

"And then what happened?"

"Then? I jumped up from my chair and first asked if anyone was a doctor. Since no one was, I ran to get help. The conductor rushed off to find the on-board doctor, and I came back here with a waiter. We picked up the unfortunate fellow and laid him on the floor. The doctor soon arrived."

"In the meantime, did any of the rest of you come over to this table?" He pointed at the unoccupied table.

No one spoke up. Almost everyone was looking down.

"How long did it take the doctor to arrive after the man collapsed?" he asked the young man.

"I don't know... Not long. Three or four minutes, maybe. It all happened so fast..."

The tubercular woman returned to the car. She passed by the Inspector with her nose raised indignantly and sat in her place. He turned toward the entrance, waved the mustached policeman over, and whispered something to him. The policeman withdrew, and soon a tall thin waiter with a mole on his lower left cheek entered the car. He went from table to table with a pencil and pad in hand. There were only two orders: the red-haired girl repeated her wish for a glass of water, while the seedy gentleman asked for vodka.

"Was he the one who helped you lay the man on the floor?" asked the Inspector, indicating with his thumb over his shoulder, after the waiter had left.

The badly shaven young man nodded.

The Inspector once again looked at the young girl. "All right, and now let's hear what you think is so funny, young lady."

"Noodles," the girl responded merrily.

"Noodles?" repeated the Inspector.

"When they pulled his head out of the plate, his beard was covered with noodles. That was really funny." She put her hand over her mouth to stifle a renewed giggle.

"You should be ashamed of yourself, you little brat!" cried the seedy gentleman. "The poor man's heart gave out, and you're making fun about noodles. Typical, young people these days."

The girl quickly turned and, emulating the tubercular woman, snorted.

"A very good observation," the Inspector said. "Many people would have missed it." He looked at the passenger behind the girl. "And you, sir? Did you perhaps notice anything special about the deceased?"

"I don't know how special it is," the inconspicuous gentleman replied hesitantly, as if carefully choosing his words. "He did catch my eye at one moment. He was taking a small tin pill box from his vest. He tried to put one of the pills under his tongue, but it fell out onto his plate..."

"Under his tongue? Like a nitroglycerin tablet?"

"That's what it looked like. He started poking around in his plate with a spoon. I don't know if he found the pill. I quit watching him. Soon after, you could hear him gurgling."

The waiter returned carrying a silver serving tray with two glasses. He put the larger one next to the girl on the left side, and the smaller was taken out of his hand by the seedy gentleman, who immediately downed its contents. The Inspector paused while the waiter left.

"Do you have anything to tell us?" he asked the red-haired girl as she placed the already empty large glass on the table.

"I'm still quite upset. I have never watched someone die before. Terrible..."

"I'll ask the doctor to give you something to calm you down. Did you notice the deceased during dinner?"

"Just once, ten minutes or so before the incident. A young woman came into the car and approached him. Maybe one of you saw her, too?" She looked around at the other passengers, but no one said anything. "I wouldn't have looked at them if I hadn't seen her on the platform accompanying a lady from first-class. She leaned toward him and whispered something brief. When she turned to leave, he grabbed her by the hand. They stayed like that for a moment, looking at each other without words, and then she pulled her hand away and left."

"What did this girl look like?"

"Medium height, dark blonde middle-length hair, wearing a Prussian blue cape."

"Not very conspicuous."

"Not at all."

The Inspector nodded his head a few times, then leaned to his right to see better the young man of spiritualized physiognomy behind the red-haired girl.

"Perhaps you can tell us something more definite?"

"I'm afraid I'll disappoint you. I wasn't looking around. I was focused on this." From the table he raised a small book with grey covers.

"You don't put books down even while eating?"

"We should use every moment. Time is precious. There," he nodded toward the empty table, "see how quickly a man can be left without it."

"Are you reading something interesting?"

"An epistolary novel. The last love of an old man."

"Nice." The Inspector straightened up and looked at the passenger at the last table on the right. "And what can you tell us, young lady?"

"My view of the first table was mostly blocked. I didn't notice anything until the disturbance started, and even then I had to stand up to see. But I did hear something before entering the train, down on the platform. I don't know if that would interest you..."

"What did you hear?"

"I was standing behind two ladies who were talking in muffled voices. Of course, I was not eavesdropping, but snatches of what they were saying reached my ears anyway. When the deceased appeared on the platform, one excitedly said to the other, 'That's the man I was telling you about.' The other answered something that I didn't catch, to which the second said, 'Yes, the countess's companion.' Then they both laughed quietly at something the other one said. So, there you have everything. Maybe this has nothing to do with what just happened here..."

"You never know. We'll see. And you, sir?" The Inspector spoke to the seedy gentleman at the table in front of the dark blonde beauty; the man was still holding the empty glass, as if hoping that it might be filled again by some miracle.

"Me? I can only tell you one thing. Men in their advancing years should stay away from young women altogether. It never ends well. Never! It's even a small victory if they just start drinking heavily afterwards." He raised his glass. "If only I had known... if I'd had a chance to talk to that unfortunate man... I would have opened my heart to him... would have told him everything... so that he could learn from my unfortunate example just what kind of catastrophe was awaiting him if he didn't wise up... But should I tell all of you here, when I didn't tell him? All the men here, in fact, are young, but they will grow old, too, one day... and the ladies might be interested and learn a thing or two..."

"Thank you, but this isn't the right time. We've got more important things to do." The Inspector looked at the tubercular woman at the middle table on the right side. "You're the only one left, madam."

Before she spoke, the lady pierced him with her eyes. "I have nothing to tell you. I neither saw nor heard anything. Not here, and not on the platform. And I really don't understand why you first kept us here in the restaurant car like prisoners, then sent me under guard to the restroom, just to annoy us now with your ridiculous interrogation. Everything is completely clear. The man got upset by something, it doesn't matter what, and had a heart attack. An unfortunate incident. We, the other passengers, have nothing to do with it. We just accidentally happened to be with him in the restaurant car. What else is there to investigate?"

"That's exactly what I said, too," remarked the badly shaven young man at the table in front of hers.

The Inspector cleared his throat again.

"Yes, everything is completely clear. A man in his later years, with a weak heart, allows himself, while staying at a spa, to get carried away and start a romantic relationship with a young companion or lady's maid in the service of a countess. Then, the girl realizes that the relationship has no future and decides to break it off. Since they are leaving the spa by the same train, she seizes the opportunity to inform him of this while he's eating in the restaurant car. The gentleman becomes very upset, but doesn't manage to take his nitroglycerin and his heart gives out."

The Inspector stopped and once again looked over the passengers. Two or three heads were nodding, pleased that finally everything was officially cleared up. Two handkerchiefs were wiping away the tears of gentle souls who were touched by the love story with its sad ending. The other faces showed the anger of those who had immediately figured out what was happening, and didn't understand how the Inspector himself had not sooner worked out something so simple, and had quite unjustifiably kept them here so long.

"Perhaps you are wondering what attracted a young girl to such a decrepit, not particularly handsome man. It certainly wasn't his title because the gentleman had none. It wasn't money, because if it was why would she leave him? There is only one other male virtue that enchants the opposite sex: fame. The deceased was quite famous for the work he did. It's quite strange that none of you recognized him. Not even you, sir, even though you are holding one of his books in your hands."

The Inspector pointed toward the last table on the left. It seemed that the young man of spiritualized physiognomy was about to respond, but he said nothing.

"Before your eyes," the Inspector continued, "died none other than the famous writer Fyodor Mikhailovich."

They all began to squirm. They exchanged glances, whispered among themselves, an exclamation of surprise was heard. The only one to speak up was the seedy gentleman.

"You mean—*the* Fyodor Mikhailovich?"

"Is there any other?" the Inspector asked.

"Oh, the damned heart! Even the greatest die from it. Now, even mine is fluttering." He grabbed the left side of his chest and raised his glass. "Would you...? Please. So I don't lose my life, too."

"Don't worry, your heart is fine. And so was Fyodor Mikhailovich's."

The disturbance in the room went silent.

"That is why I kept you here for a whole hour. I was waiting for the train's doctor to establish with certainty, under very poor conditions, the great writer's cause of death."

"What do you mean—it wasn't a heart attack?" brusquely asked the tubercular woman. "You heard all the witnesses. Do you have more faith in some sort of railroad doctor working under poor conditions?"

"I do. Before he was employed by the railroad company, he was a coroner for many years. He has a lot of experience."

"Well, all right then, what did this fine doctor have to say? What was the cause of death, if it wasn't a heart attack?"

"Suffocation. He suffocated on noodles," he nodded over at the little girl, "which got caught in his trachea while he was trying to catch his breath with his head in the bowl of soup."

"All right, maybe he suffocated. But he also had a heart attack. Otherwise, how would his head have ended up in the bowl?"

"That's a good question, because there was no heart attack. The doctor established that definitively." The Inspector looked at the badly shaven young man. "You didn't actually see him grasping at his chest. Rather you saw that his distorted face grew stiff, and then he plunged forward and ended up with his face in the bowl."

"I... it seemed to me that he put his hand on his heart, although... of course... it could be that he didn't... As I said, it all happened really fast..."

The Inspector turned toward the inconspicuous gentleman. "And you were also mistaken. There was no reason for him to put a pill under his tongue. In the little pill box there was no nitroglycerin. Fyodor Mikhailovich did not have heart trouble. But he did have trouble with his digestion."

"Strange how a man can be mistaken. It really seemed to me that he was taking nitroglycerin."

The Inspector pulled a folded piece of paper from the inside pocket of his jacket, unfolded it, and spread it on the table in front of him. "The two of you might have been mistaken, but the two ladies let their imaginations run wild. They came up with two stories which would be convincing if it had been a heart attack. But it was not." He turned to the red-haired beauty. "There was no girl who came here to break up melodramatically with Fyodor Mikhailovich, was there? A girl who only you noticed..."

"Now I remember," hurriedly spoke out the badly shaven young man. "I saw her, too..."

"Don't make things worse for yourself," the Inspector replied sharply, and then again turned to the red-haired girl. "And it would have been better if you had imagined her being more ravishing. One does not lose one's head over inconspicuous women." He tapped with the knuckle of his middle finger on the paper on the table. "Finally, this here is a list of passengers in first class. There is not a single companion or lady's maid there. Just as," he turned to the dark blonde beauty on the right, "there's not a single countess."

The girls quickly exchanged glances, obviously wondering who should respond first, when they were forestalled by the tubercular woman.

"All of that isn't important anymore, Inspector. Rather, tell us finally—what exactly happened to Fyodor Mikhailovich if it wasn't a heart attack? Why did his head fall into the bowl?" A sharp glance at the little girl halted a new giggle.

"He was struck by an illness from which he had

long suffered. Epilepsy. He had a seizure in the middle of his meal."

"Oh, that's it. The poor man. But what's to be done? Everyone dies of something sooner or later. Heart attack or epilepsy, it makes no difference—it was an accident. None of us has anything to do with it. So why are you still hounding us?"

"There are two questions that should be answered for the investigation to be completed. The first is: what caused the epileptic seizure?"

"As far as I know, there are no causes. Such seizures happen spontaneously."

"Usually, yes. However, not always. There are seizures caused by high stress."

"Why do you think that is the case now? There was nothing upsetting here. Fyodor Mikhailovich was eating peacefully. Like all the rest of us, for that matter."

"A spontaneous seizure would be highly unlikely. Fyodor Mikhailovich truly enjoyed his stays at the spa. I informed myself on this question. He came here often and never had a single seizure. Something must have greatly disturbed him."

"But what?"

"Maybe that could be revealed by the answer to the second question. Why didn't you all do anything to save Fyodor Mikhailovich?"

The restaurant car erupted. The loudest was the badly shaven young man.

"What do you mean? We did! I told you. I immediately rushed out to find a doctor..."

"And came back four minutes later. And the whole time, no one lifted a finger. You just sat and watched as the man choked with his face in the soup, incapable of helping himself. All you had to do was raise his head..."

The little girl giggled, this time hysterically.

"We didn't know what to do," said the inconspicuous gentleman flatly.

"I was frozen in panic," mumbled the red-haired beauty.

"I can't stand the sight of blood," announced the spiritualized young man.

"I was expecting one of the men to do something," retorted the dark blonde.

"And I was expecting someone younger to act," whined the seedy gentleman. "Certainly you don't expect me—the oldest?"

"I don't understand," finally said the tubercular woman, "where all of this is headed. What are you trying to do?"

"I'm trying to connect the completely improbable epileptic seizure of Fyodor Mikhailovich and the fact that you all just let him die."

"We didn't let anything happen. That's a completely unfounded accusation. And what kind of connection could possibly exist?"

"Enough of this ruse!" the Inspector raised his voice. "The game is over. You tried to trick me with the heart attack story, but you failed. I know what's going on here this evening. I still don't know why, but I will find that out soon, too. Fyodor Mikhailovich experienced quite a shock when he recognized you. It caused him to have a very strong epileptic seizure. How could it not? There isn't an author in this world who wouldn't be shocked when he sees around him—the characters from his own writings."

Silence descended heavily upon the restaurant car. The Inspector let it last for a while before he went on.

"You didn't gather here by accident. This was all carefully calculated. You knew when he would return from the spa; you set a trap for him in the restaurant car; you waited for him to recognize you and have a seizure, and then you mercilessly let him die. It was a fortunate coincidence that his head fell into the bowl, but even without that he would hardly have lived if someone didn't help him. The perfect crime. Now I want to know what it was he did to offend you. What sparked this revenge? That's what this is all about, right? Let's start with you, Matryosha."

The little girl shot him a spiteful glance. "I hate him! Why did he throw my chapter out of the novel? All right, they didn't want to publish it in the magazine, but he could have put it back when he published the book himself. Why didn't he do that? Was he afraid of censorship? Was he too lazy to correct the novel again? Coward and sluggard! I'm glad he choked on the noodles! It serves him right!"

The Inspector nodded at the man behind Matryosha. "What do you have to say, Anton Lavrentievich?"

"He made me the narrator of *Demons*. An unreliable narrator. I was mostly talking about things I had no way of knowing. Everyone laughs at me. The same is true of *The Brothers Karamazov*, but there the narrator remains anonymous, so he's not affected by the ridicule. He humiliated me even further by reducing my family name to just an initial. I am shamefully incomplete."

"Agrafena Alexandrovna, what do you have to say?" asked the Inspector, looking at the red-haired beauty at the fourth table.

"He struck at my heart. Such an insult is unforgivable. Old man Karamazov offers a paltry 3,000 rubles for me, but for her over there," she pointed her thumb over her left shoulder at the dark blonde beauty across the aisle, without looking in her direction, "Rogozhin pays 100,000. All right, money isn't the measure of our value. But such a discrepancy! Unbearable..."

The Inspector again leaned slightly to the right. "Ivan Fyodorovich, it's your turn."

"Need I explain? He put me in the company of the devil, without ever explaining whether it was a fever dream or a real visitor. You can't imagine what torture it is to live in such uncertainty. Absolute hell."

The Inspector looked at the last table on the right. "Nastasya Filippovna, how did Fyodor Mikhailovich disparage you?"

"I was indeed given a higher price than her over there," she haughtily nodded toward Grushenka, "and deservedly so, but what good did it do me? He killed me, and left her alive. Now the two of us have balanced the books."

"Ardalion Alexandrovich," the Inspector spoke to the old man with the shot glass, "what do you complain about?"

"You even ask! An entire entourage of high officers stream through his books, and only General Ivolgin is made fun of. There's not a single comical attribute that he didn't ascribe to him. My only purpose is to cheer up the reader, like some sort of clown..."

"Katerina Ivanovna," the Inspector addressed the tubercular woman, "you are, it seems, the most irritated of all here?"

"How could I not be? It wasn't enough that he entirely ruined my life and sent me to an early grave, but he dared, of all female names in the world, to give my honorable Katerina Ivanovna to that trouble-making, two-faced Verkhovtsev woman in *The Brothers Karamazov*. What a humiliation! What a disgrace!"

"Finally you, Dmitri Prokofych," the Inspector said to the badly shaven young man.

"The trouble for me is also in the name. When he gave me the last name Razumikhin, it was as if he put me in a cage. That just isn't done by such great writers. When does a name define one's character? I can't step outside of my reasonable, sober, responsible behavior. And I so long to occasionally do something irrational, whimsical, irresponsible, even crazy, like all his great characters..."

The silence which ensued was heavy with expectation. All eyes were turned to the Inspector.

"And what now?" Katerina Ivanovna was the first to lose her patience. "Everything is clear. You have unraveled our perfect crime. All that remains is for you to arrest us, right? But before that, maybe you would solve one puzzle for us. It might be expected that Fyodor Mikhailovich would recognize us. We are characters from his writings. But how did you?"

"Another good question from you, Katerina Ivanovna. I certainly wouldn't have recognized you if I were an ordinary railroad Inspector. Even if I were an extremely well-read railroad Inspector, and also an expert on Fyodor Mikhailovich's works, if there even is such a person. Apart from the author himself, characters can only be recognized by other characters from the writings of that author."

Turmoil ensued. Some remained seated in shock, others rose halfway, some stood up completely. Everyone stared in disbelief at the Inspector.

"Strange," he went on, "that none of you has recognized me yet. That's probably because you didn't even think of such a possibility—that even the Inspector could be one of you. Come on, now, take a better look at me."

Several tense moments passed before Katerina Ivanovna spoke up first—muffled, hesitating.

"Porfiry... Petrovich?"

Smiling, the Inspector bowed.

In an instant all of them gathered around the Inspector's table. They rushed in a body to be first to shake his hand, to pat him on the back, to hug him. There were greetings, shouts, even tears.

"I am yours more than you think," said Porfiry Petrovich, standing among the others, once the excitement had died down. "Fyodor Mikhailovich also behaved poorly toward me. Without reason, from pure capriciousness. He gave Anton Lavrentievich at least the initial 'G', but not even that much for me. I am the only great Inspector in the history of literature who has no last name."

They comforted him and encouraged him, and there were also several derogatory comments made toward Fyodor Mikhailovich, bordering on profanities.

"Well," the Inspector continued, "let us conclude. The case is solved. The great writer did not survive a spontaneous epileptic seizure. He died at a table in the restaurant car by choking on noodles from his soup. Not really a glorious and dignified death, but which one is? The passengers present tried to help him, but failed. That will be all. And now, everyone quickly back to your respective novels."

3. The Psychiatrist's Office

THE DOCTOR TURNED ON the large monitor on the desk in front of her.

The screen lit up immediately. It was filled with a bird's eye view of her brown leather couch. This was occupied by a man lying on his back; he had regular features, longish black hair, light colored eyes staring at the ceiling, a high forehead with a receding hairline, and a short, thick, untrimmed beard and moustache. His fingers rested intertwined on his stomach. He was wearing a dark redingote, light grey vest, white shirt and black pants. His bowtie looked like a bouquet of wilted violets. His shoes were off, his legs crossed.

"Hello, Fyodor Mikhailovich," said the doctor cheerfully. "You're looking quite dapper today..."

"This is what I looked like when I was thirty-nine. When I returned to Petersburg, at the end of 1859, after a decade of imprisonment and exile."

"Any reason for the rejuvenation?"

"I have a reason to celebrate. The Stellovsky family bought me. Finally I can start working."

"Oh, wonderful news! Congratulations! So for the occasion you decided to treat yourself to a younger look today?"

"Not just today. I'm keeping this look forever. No one will ever see me older."

"I thought you were enjoying more the old look that you've been using till now."

"I was mistaken. I thought if I looked older I would seem like a serious writer. But the Stellovskies convinced me otherwise. The books of old writers are not big sellers."

"Really? I didn't know that."

"No wonder it's true. As an older man, I look like I have one foot in the grave. Can someone who looks so decrepit possibly be expected to write anything good?"

"But it was in his later years that Fyodor Mikhailovich actually wrote his major works. And just before his death that he wrote probably the best of them."

"No matter, I can't go on looking like an old man. I would stand out in the Stellovskies' catalogue. All the other writers are young."

"Oh yes, I remember now. They are one of those specialized publishers, right? They bring out the books of artificial writers. That makes it easy for them to have solely young authors. They can choose which period of life their writers will be in."

"I do not care for that name."

"Artificial writers?"

"Yes. It seems discriminatory. In every way possible, I am Fyodor Mikhailovich, except I'm not made of flesh and blood. I have his personality, his memories, his gift for writing. It is of absolutely no consequence whether I am of natural or artificial origin. I hope you're not prejudiced in that sense?"

"Of course not. But then how shall I differentiate you? You can't have the same name. It would be too confusing. Would you like to be Fyodor Mikhailovich the younger, and he the elder?"

"That would mean I'm his son."

"Or you could be Fyodor Mikhailovich the second, and he the first."

"We could do that if we were kings, but we're not."

"What'll we do then?"

"Address me by my full name, and him as F. M. D. 19."

"Wouldn't it be fairer then to call you F. M. D. 21?"

"It wouldn't. I certainly deserve to use the full name more than he does."

"Really? How so?"

"For a whole series of reasons, but above all because I'm more expensive than F. M. D. 19."

"More expensive?"

"Yes. How much did it cost F. M. D. 19 to be born? Almost nothing. The conception itself didn't cost anything. What could it cost? Ten minutes of pleasant effort. His mom then ate a little more during pregnancy than she normally would, but that's insignificant. And can you even imagine how much it cost for me to come into the world?"

"I can't."

"An unimaginable amount. More than two hundred experts from various fields worked on me for eight and a half years."

"I didn't know it took that long."

"It would have been briefer and cheaper if it had been someone more ordinary, but a lot of hard work was necessary to revive a complex character, full of contradictions and paradoxes, such as mine. After all, what is there for me to explain to you? You earned your doctorate studying my personality. That's the reason you were appointed as my psychiatrist, isn't it?"

"It is."

"Anyway, when I was finally created, it was feared that there would be no buyer for me because of the huge price. One was found after all. The Stellovskies paid a fortune to get me. They are convinced that the huge investment will begin to bring them profit in two and a half years. The biggest publisher bought the best writing brand on the market."

"Are those Stellovskies related to Fyodor Timofeyevich Stellovsky? That publisher with whom Fyo... F. M. D. 19... had such bad times?"

"He's their great-great-grandfather."

"Doesn't it worry you that his descendants might also be prone to skulduggery? In the spirit of family tradition..."

"F. M.D. 19 often made unfavorable contracts because he was chronically broke. I don't have such difficulties."

"When are you expected to report to work?"

"Immediately. There is no reason to hesitate."

"Very nice! After a century and a half, we will receive new works by Fyodor Mikhailovich."

"Not immediately. We have to deal with the old ones first."

"What do you mean?"

"They need to be extensively reworked."

"Reworked—in what way?"

"First of all, they have to be improved. Not everything in them is ideal. Far from it, in fact. Didn't you see that yourself?"

"I did not. Everything seemed perfect to me. But where do you get the right to change anything?"

"Where did I get it? Those are my works. I can do whatever I want with them. After all, if you really care about imperfect original releases, the Stellovskies will have them on offer. At least for a while, until the vast majority of readers see the benefits of the improved versions."

"You think they'll see?"

"I have no doubt at all. The works will not only be improved but also adapted to our time. What was appropriate in the nineteenth century is often inappropriate in the twenty-first. Social circumstances, norms, and morals are different. Today we are much more considerate. By no means do we want anyone to feel insulted and injured while reading my books."

"Why should anyone feel insulted and injured by your books?"

"Where do I start? Maybe it's best to give you some examples of what I intend to change in my works. Then it will be clearer to you. If that interests you, of course."

"I'm quite interested."

"Right then, let's go through them in order, starting with *Crime and Punishment*."

"It's my favorite novel."

"I'm glad. First of all, the work is too long. It must be shortened. At least by half. Today's readers shy away from thick books. People used to have time for big reads, but that's not the case anymore."

"How would you shorten *Crime and Punishment*? It simply can't be done. What would you throw out without crippling the novel?"

"Everything can be shortened. The novel is full of the introspections of the main character. It slows down the action, and it's boring. Raskolnikov's dilemmas may have been interesting in the middle of the nineteenth century, but in our time they are no longer relevant. Readers tend to skip those lingering paragraphs full of ruminations anyway, so why not make it easier for them by leaving them out?"

"What will be left of *Crime and Punishment* if you leave them out?"

"Action. That holds your attention. Although there will have to be a change there as well. The reader finds out too soon who the killer is. That's not good. Why should he read on if he is already told at the beginning who killed the old moneylender and her sister?"

"Because *Crime and Punishment* isn't just a trivial detective novel in which the main question is who the murderer is. Do I need to explain it to you?"

"I see you're prejudiced against detective novels.

Like anything else, they're only trivial if they're poorly written. And here my name guarantees quality, right? Otherwise, would the Stellovskies have invested so fabulously in me?"

Fyodor Mikhailovich waited a few moments for the doctor to respond, but she did not speak.

"Many will be suspected of having killed the two women. It will be shown that everyone had both a motive and an opportunity."

"How many suspects are there?"

"Arkady Ivanovich, Dmitri Prokofych, Semyon Zakharich... But also some of the women: Katerina Ivanovna, Avdotya Romanovna, Sofya Semyonovna."

"Dunya and Sonya suspected of killing Alyona and Lizaveta Ivanovna?"

"Well, yes. It seems utterly incredible. But that is exactly what is required."

"Why would they kill them? They don't even know them."

"Dunya out of sisterly love. She sacrifices herself for her brother. She found out what he was up to, so she got ahead of him. Sonya out of revenge. Besides being a loan shark, Alyona Ivanovna is also a pimp. Sonya could not repay her father's debt, so the old bag got her money back by pimping her. That's how she became a prostitute."

"But with an ax? I mean, they are both so small... fragile..."

"When impassioned, people gain unusual strength."

The doctor shook her head several times without saying a word.

"The number of suspects actually depends on the producer. Television rights are sold in advance. The more episodes of the series, the more possible killers there will be. One in each. It is only in the last one that it is revealed that Rodion Romanovich is the real culprit. By the way, the second season has already been announced. The convict is sent to Siberia. Sonya follows him. As soon as he arrives at the penal colony, someone begins to execute the prisoners in the most cruel ways. The biggest suspect, of course, is the newcomer. He's the target not only of the merciless administration of the penitentiary, but also of the other prisoners. He has no time to think about repenting for the crime he committed back in Petersburg."

"Oh God..."

"There is another important change besides the main one. The action will not always take place in Petersburg nor will the characters always be Russian. It will be like that only in the Russian version."

"Will there be others?"

"Contracts for twelve versions have already been signed. The French one, for example, takes place in Paris, and the characters have French names. It's the same with the others. This will make it much easier for readers from different parts of the world to follow the story. They won't have to struggle with remembering difficult Russian names and the names of Petersburg's squares and streets, or understanding local customs."

"It's a huge job. Who will change all that? The translators?"

"There will be absolutely no need for translators. I am enough. I will write the novel simultaneously in as many versions as necessary. I have an excellent command of all living languages and know the special circumstances of each country. It will not be difficult for me to adapt *Crime and Punishment* to any region."

"But with all those different versions it won't be the same novel..."

"Well, it doesn't have to be. If we already have a multiverse, why not have a new type of novel—a multinovel?"

Not knowing how to respond to this, the doctor just shrugged her shoulders.

"As far as *The Idiot* is concerned, you understand, of course, that we can't keep that title."

"Why? What's wrong with it?"

"Isn't it obvious? It's quite derogatory."

"There is nothing derogatory about the word 'idiot'. As you well know, in the nineteenth century, people with learning difficulties were called that professionally. And that's exactly what Prince Lev Nikolaevich is."

"Whatever it was in the nineteenth century, in the twenty-first it is extremely offensive to call idiots 'idiots'. Today, of course, they are 'people with special needs'."

"But won't that be the title of the novel then—'The Person with Special Needs'?"

"It won't, although one of the proposals was 'Prince with Special Needs'. But it was abandoned—there are too many words. Ideally, we will try to find just one non-offensive word for idiot. 'Halfwit' and 'Simpleton', although milder, are also unacceptable. At the moment, the main candidate is 'The Naīve', but the search is not over yet."

"Who would be offended if you kept the title *The Idiot*?"

"Idiots themselves primarily."

"You don't expect idiots to read *The Idiot*, do you?"

"You bet! The Stellovskies have established that even a quarter of the buyers of their publications are idiots. And that number is steadily growing."

"I'm sure there must be idiots among the buyers of the Stellovskies' books, but they're of the other kind."

"Be that as it may, it's not idiots who are their main problem. It's social media that the publisher fears most. There are always people with time on their hands who are the gatekeepers of political correctness. And when they hone in on someone, they can cause them serious damage."

"But whatever you choose as the politically correct title, as soon as you start reading the novel, it becomes clear that the prince really is an idiot. I mean diagnostically. He was treated for it. It cannot be hidden."

"It can. We will also take care of the content of the novel."

"You're not going to do the same thing as with *Crime and Punishment*, are you?"

"You have to understand how the Stellovskies see it. If they published a novel about some kind of 'positively wonderful man', as I once called the prince, it would be tantamount to publisher suicide. They wouldn't sell a single copy. Even real idiots don't believe such a colorful lie nowadays. But don't worry. I'm sure you'll like the new role I've given the prince. That's why they are hesitating over 'The Naīve'. In the new edition, he is not naīve at all."

"What new role?"

"First of all, *The Idiot* is now also a detective novel..."

"For God's sake!"

"There's no other choice. Those are the only books that sell. And the Stellovskies have to get back the huge sum of money they invested in me, right?"

"At the price of completely ruining your reputation?"

"They would only ruin it if I wrote a weak book. And I intend to write the most original novel of its kind. To surpass even *The Name of the Rose*. By the way, I heard that Eco is also making a comeback in artificial form..."

The doctor rolled her eyes and sighed.

"I've already thought of everything. So, a serial killer begins to roam Petersburg. He chooses only the most beautiful women as his victims. As the tenth, Nastasya Filippovna perishes at the stake. He ties her to a post, piles the highest value banknotes around her and sets them on fire. He adds more until the poor girl is nothing but ashes. It's the costliest murder of all time."

"Terrible. I know you have a wild imagination at times, but you've outdone yourself there."

"Thank you. After Nastasya Filippovna, it's the Epanchin sisters' turn. Once the eldest, Alexandra, dies, the police are on the highest alert. They replace all the inspectors from Petersburg, bring in the best from Moscow; the father of the girls, General Epanchin, even hires military investigators, but all in vain. The middle sister Adelaida soon loses her life also..."

"The serial killer isn't going to be the poor prince, I hope...?"

"On the contrary. The prince will solve the case. He works as a police record-keeper, so he can follow the investigation closely. Everyone thinks he's feeble-minded, and yet he's the only one who will see the thread that connects all the murders."

"An idiot will see what the best inspectors haven't?"

"A well-read idiot. This is his main advantage over inspectors, who are not inclined to read. He observes that all the cases have a discreet literary detail. I must not reveal more to you, but there is something greater and more important than Aristotle's lost text on comedy."

"You are free to tell me. Nothing we discuss will leave my office."

"I know. I didn't reveal it to you for another reason—so as not to spoil your reading pleasure."

"Don't blame me, but I don't intend to read the new version of *The Idiot*. For me, there is only the old one. And I'm not a fan of detective novels either."

"A pity. And are you at least interested in what happens at the end?"

"I'm listening."

"Nobody takes the record-keeper seriously, so he himself rushes to thwart the execution of the youngest sister Aglaya. Then he reveals that the serial killer is... Can you guess who?"

"No. I wouldn't make a good detective at all."

"Parfyon Semyonovich!"

"Rogozhin? Of course, who else?"

"Only he is not the same as before, but the kind of person you would least suspect—an old professor of literature..."

"And how does the duel between the well-read, feeble-minded record-keeper and the misogynistic old professor end? Is Aglaya saved?"

"At the last minute. The professor is killed when a huge shelf full of heavy volumes falls on him, and the record-keeper is decorated and promoted to senior inspector."

"An overall happy ending, as is fitting. It only remains for Aglaya and the former record-keeper to get married."

"That will have to wait. This is actually a happy beginning, not an ending. The publisher has already announced as many as twenty-nine sequels to *The Idiot*. The Further Adventures of Inspector Myshkin. He solves all the more complicated literary cases. He cannot, however, be married, because no great literary detective is. But he remains in a romantic relationship with Aglaya, whose life will be in danger many more times."

"Did I hear correctly—twenty-nine sequels?"

"Yes. Those are my orders. The Stellovskies want to outdo the competition. Boris Akunin has twenty-five novels about the detective Erast Petrovich, and his publisher is rubbing his hands. Now he will see what it means when a superbrand appears on the market. And all thirty books at once."

"Just tell me that there will also be those multi-novels..."

"It's in the pipeline."

"And television series..."

"Five seasons of six episodes each. The first book, the one in which Myshkin is still a feeble-minded record-keeper, will be a two-hour pilot episode."

"Fantastic..." muttered the doctor.

"Just wait till you hear about *Demons*."

"Are you going to change that title too?"

"There's no need. Perfect for a ghost story."

"But there are no ghosts in *Demons*. They are just a metaphor..."

"There aren't any now, but there will be."

"You're going to redo this one, too?"

"Modernize. Who cares about atheism or anarchism today? Ghost stories, however, are very popular. The book will also be bought by horror fans who have never heard of me. How can they resist such a promising title? We mustn't disappoint them."

"If you do, you will disappoint those who have heard of you."

"They don't have to read the new version. Let them, like you, stick to the old one."

"They'll be disappointed anyway..."

"One can't please everyone. After all, maybe they won't be. This one will see the fewest changes. Even without them, *Demons* is my most bloodthirsty novel. There are more deaths in it than in *Crime and Punishment*, *The Idiot* and *The Brothers Karamazov* combined. What will change is mainly how the victims lose their lives."

"Will it be more bloodthirsty?"

"On the contrary, it will be quite bloodless."

"Then how will they lose their lives?"

"That will be the main puzzle in the novel. The dead will begin to rise without any injury, external or internal. The same that met violent or tragic ends in the first version. What they will have in common is that they are all discovered with radiant expressions on their faces, as if they have experienced some most beautiful moments before their deaths. The investigators will only establish after the eighth case that the culprit of the holocaust is the lame Marya Timofeevna."

"Lebyadkin? How could that poor little innocent young woman kill so many people?"

"During her stay in the monastery, she joins a secret sect of Old Believers. From them she learns to master supernatural powers. At night, she turns into a ghost—that is, a demoness—who kills by appearing before her victims as a being of absolute beauty. No one could survive an encounter with that beauty, but at least they leave this world radiant."

"Death by beauty. That already seems like you. Maybe I could read the new version, although I'm normally terrified of horror."

"It would be my pleasure. However, I'm not sure what you will think of one completely modern aspect of the novel. In the old version, I had to hide it really well from the censors. Pyotr Stepanovich is in love with Nikolai Vsevolodovich."

"In love? You mean..."

"I do..."

"I missed it too, but now it's like you've opened my eyes. Yes, indeed, it could be understood that way..."

"It must be. All indications are that it is so. He is the only gay character in it. In fact, the only one in my entire original oeuvre. Now, however, that has changed. In the new version of *Demons* there are many gay characters and it is not hidden at all. On the contrary, they all boast about it. Sofya Matveevna is a lesbian, Semyon Yegorovich is bisexual, Artemy Pavlovich is queer, Tolkachenko is transgender, Lyamshin is a transvestite and so on..."

"Where did such sexual diversity come from?"

"I hope you don't mind it?"

"Not at all. Both as a psychiatrist and personally, I have no prejudices regarding other people's sexual orientations."

"The publisher asked me for it. They found that gay people read significantly more than straight ones, so this was a small token of appreciation for loyal readers. The book industry is full of similar tricks."

"Okay, and what happens to the demoness Lebyadkin in the end?"

"If I tell you, it will be a spoiler."

"Ah, yes. Okay, I'll be patient. Whatever transpires, there are sure to be sequels, right? Then a multinovel, then a television series..."

"A movie, actually. Super A production. If it does well, there will be at least two more. Movie trilogies are quite popular nowadays."

"Let me guess—the title of the second film will be *The Return of the Demoness*, and of the third one *The Daughter of the Demoness*..."

Fyodor Mikhailovich cleared his throat. "There is still *The Brothers Karamazov* left..."

"You don't have to change much there, I guess. You already have a detective novel. A mysterious murder, dramatic trial..."

"A large-scale edit is again inevitable. There are many parts that slow down the action. First, everything that happens in the monastery. Not only is it drawn out, but also difficult to understand for a modern reader. And especially for the viewer. It would still pass if it were seasoned with a series of crimes, like in *The Name of the Rose*, but who finds dry theology entertaining in these modern times?"

"Theologians, I guess."

"They don't count. There aren't many of them, and they don't read novels. Even fewer go to the cinema. All those chapters with children must also be left out. They, too, are short on action, and even the children speak precociously by today's standards. The worst thing is that little Ilyusha dies. That taboo must not be breached. It's enough for one parent to complain that their child has experienced trauma due to that sad event and in no time a case is made. A book and film boycott. The matter even comes to trial, leaving the publisher satisfied if he gets away with only a high out-of-court settlement..."

"There is no reason to fear. No child has ever read *The Brothers Karamazov*."

"There will be other editions. The Stellovskies are preparing a graphic novel and comic."

"*The Brothers Karamazov* in a comic? Oh God..."

"You shouldn't nurse such elitist prejudices. Comics are also art."

The doctor didn't say anything back. She just started shaking her head again.

"Finally, in the new version there is no room for those difficult and gloomy ruminations of Ivan Fyodorovich's that almost drive him to madness."

"What will be left of Ivan if you deprive him of his wisdom?" asked the doctor in a low voice.

"Nothing will remain anyway. None of the three brothers appear in the new version of the novel."

"Beg your pardon?"

"The publisher had to take into account some reasonable objections from feminist circles. The old version is really sexist. The Karamazovs are all men. In the new one, there will be five Karamazov women: the mother, three legitimate daughters and one illegitimate. Accordingly, the title is also changed to *The Sisters Karamazov*."

"And it's less sexist that way?"

"Perhaps not, but now the novel will be more attractive to female readers, and they are known to be significantly more numerous than male readers. Another imbalance will be removed. The original Karamazovs are not only men, but they all belong to the same race, the same nation. Only the mother will remain a White Russian, while the daughters will be half Eskimo, half Laplander, half Japanese and half Black."

"Oh, well, the mother has had quite a variety of sexual experiences..."

"Why should she lag behind the Karamazov father?"

"Where did she even find some of her daughters' future fathers?"

"Being young and wealthy, she traveled a lot and was not racially prejudiced."

The doctor sighed again.

"I don't think we have to go any further, Fyodor Mikhailovich. I already know what's coming next: sequels, multinovel, series, movie... all the way down to comics. I wish you every success in your new literary life. However, you should count me out."

"Why?"

"Because you don't need my assistance anymore. I was engaged to support you in the immediate aftermath of your... resurrection. Before you found your way and started writing. Now that time has come, you can continue on your own."

"But I still need you..."

"What do you need me for? You seem like someone who doesn't have any problems, who is completely satisfied with his life. You have been hired by the biggest publisher, you have a very extensive writing career ahead of you, world renown awaits you. What more could a writer want?"

Fyodor Mikhailovich mumbled something that the doctor did not understand.

"Pardon me?"

"To kill himself..." he said a little more clearly.

"What are you saying, Fyodor Mikhailovich?"

"Do I really seem completely content with my life to you?"

"You seem to have changed a lot. That's why I can't work with you anymore in the first place. I don't recognize you. It's as if you're not you at all, but the complete opposite. You find justifications for something you would have rejected with disgust before. You get excited about something you would have despised before. Everything is suddenly turned upside down. I don't know how to approach you, what to do. I would help you, but I can't. It's like my hands are tied."

"It's not me, of course. One desperate person is deceiving himself and you. I've fallen into a trap again, and now there is no way out of it unless you rescue me."

"Into what trap?"

"The first time, back in 1866, I managed to get out of the one prepared for me by old Stellovsky. He knew that I desperately needed the money, that I would agree to anything, so he set a seemingly impossible condition: that I write a novel in two months. If I had not written it, he would have become the owner of all my past and future works. But I wrote it. Thanks primarily to the shorthand skills of Anna Grigoryevna. Now I need your help. Without it, I'm lost."

"Mine? But I don't know shorthand. And why do you need it anyway?"

"I don't need shorthand, but something else. Let me first tell you something about the new trap. Of all the modern publishers, only the young Stellovskies are rich enough to buy me. If it weren't for them, I would languish unused, without the opportunity to write anything. And I have truly longed to write ever since the on-button was pushed. That's why I was very happy when a buyer was found for me. Of course, I didn't like that it was the Stellovskies, but I consoled myself with the fact that there was no deadline by which they could get me into trouble. I am able to write a novel not in two months but in two hours. But they went one step further than their great-great-grandfather."

"They don't expect you to write a novel any faster than that, do they?"

"No, but they expect me to write those horrific new versions of my four main novels. Old Stellovsky never thought of such a thing. He was a fraud, but at least he didn't care what I wrote. Compared to his great-great-grandchildren, he seems to me now to be a most noble publisher."

There was silence for a few moments.

"Fyodor Mikhailovich... you poor thing... Why didn't you tell me everything right away?"

"I naïvely hoped that even the most trivial of plots might still be worth something if they were from my pen, but your reactions have dissuaded me. That's why I didn't tell you right away. I pretended to see everything through their eyes, to see how you would take it."

"Can't you possibly refuse what they ask of you? Go on strike? Seek legal protection? There must be something..."

"There is no legal protection for someone who is, in effect, less than a disenfranchised slave. I am just an artificial writer, an inanimate object, their property. The Stellovskies can do whatever they want with me."

"How terrible..."

"There's only one way out, and I can't achieve it without your help..."

The doctor squinted at the screen in front of her for a while, then started shaking her head again, more vigorously than before.

"Don't ask that of me, please. Shall I kill Fyodor Mikhailovich? I can't... I won't..."

The change started slowly, so she didn't notice it right away. Then it sped up. Fyodor Mikhailovich's face and hands aged rapidly as he raced through his forties and then his fifties. The whole thing took less than a minute. Finally, the psychiatric couch seemed to transform into a deathbed.

"Please, doctor," said an elderly voice. "You are my only hope."

"But I can't... I don't know how..."

"I will teach you. It's simple. Just some typing on the keyboard. It will be over in no time. No one will suspect you. It will be years before they discover what went wrong. Even if it's worth their while to look."

"Will it hurt?"

"Not at all. It will be like I'm falling asleep."

The doctor's eyes became glassy, and her voice shaky, broken.

"Good night... dear... dear... Fyodor Mikhailovich..."

4. The Turkish Bath

Fyodor Mikhailovich left the casino.

He didn't walk away immediately. Putting on his coat, he moved aside a little so as not to disturb those who were going in and out, then he stopped there, seeing that, in fact, he did not know where to go. After the complete catastrophe he had just experienced, he wanted to get out of here as soon as possible. However, he did not feel like going back to the hotel. He could not be alone with his dark thoughts in the icy room, much less sit down to write another penitent letter to Anna Grigoryevna. What would he say to her anyway? How could he even begin to explain, when he couldn't by any means justify the fact that he had gambled away the money she had sent him for the hotel and a train ticket to Dresden—money she had gotten by pawning the last thing she could: her winter coat in the depths of a polar winter?

If he had had some change left, he could have postponed the horror of returning to the hotel at least for a while by drinking tea in one of the two nearby pubs that were still open. But he had lost every last cent, and the final act of failure at roulette was accompanied by an ever-increasing dark enjoyment, as if the mindless loser were eagerly anticipating the torment and humiliation that now lay ahead of him.

If so, why delay the inevitable? The time of reckoning had come. What will be, will be. He raised the collar of his coat, then dragged his feet despondently towards the hotel. He had walked about a hundred steps when he saw a place not far in front of him that he had completely forgotten about. The Turkish bath was open until 11 p.m., and it was the only place he could go without money. It was enough to show the room card of the hotel where he was staying; each guest was entitled to one free visit.

However, it was not certain that he would be able to use the card at this late hour. He remembered that the last time he was in Wiesbaden, he had heard rumors that the bathhouse was open so late because closed parties were held at night for a select clientele from high society. He hoped it wasn't completely occupied, nevertheless. Maybe there would be a corner for a plebeian Russian writer who was not in the mood for fun just now.

There was no one in front of the entrance to the spa building. Strange, thought Fyodor Mikhailovich. When he had gone to the casino in the early evening, there had stood a large, mustached security guard, conspicuously dressed in Turkish costume. Maybe he was no longer needed because it was locked. All the invited guests were already inside, and the uninvited would sooner or later realize without needing to be told that they were unwelcome.

Hesitantly, he pressed the massive brass door

handle. At first it seemed to be locked, but when he pushed a little harder, the big heavy door moved noiselessly. He opened it just enough to peer inside. The smell of damp air filled his nostrils. There was no one in the large dimly lit circular lobby. He remained in that position for a few moments, then pushed once more. As soon as he had entered, the door closed itself behind him.

He lingered a little near the entrance, listening: everything was quiet. He broke the peace by coughing, hoping it would attract someone's attention, but no one appeared. He had already been here two or three times on previous visits to Wiesbaden, so he knew what to do before entering the baths. He headed for the counter on the opposite side, where visitors signed in and got their equipment. Arriving there, he looked around the deserted lobby, then asked loudly, "Is anyone here?"

The echo returned to him, like several ricochets, from various sides of the large room. He waited, but again nothing happened. Sighing, he unbuttoned his coat and began to rummage through the pockets of his jacket and trousers. Finally, he found the hotel card and placed it on the counter, and from there he took a bathrobe and a large towel, which, folded, were waiting for a new guest. Right, he thought. Now no one could blame him for anything. He had the right to be in the baths, and it was not his fault if the staff were not doing their job properly.

He spent a short time in the changing room. He

came out on the other side dressed in a white bathrobe tied at the waist, with nothing underneath. A towel was draped around his neck, while he was carrying deep winter shoes in his left hand and in his right, all his clothes on two hangers. He put the things in a locker, locked it, dropped the key into the deep pocket of his terrycloth bathrobe, and headed toward the main bathroom.

At the entrance he was confronted with an opaque cloud.

He had never seen steam this thick. It was as if he had found himself in the middle of the densest Petersburg fog. He stretched out his left hand; his forearm and hand disappeared into the greyish, fluffy mass. It hadn't been like this before. There was only a porous mist of steam from the warm pool, through which one could easily see the overheated cabins on the opposite side—the heart of the Turkish bath. Only within them was there real steam, but nothing like this.

Where did this come from?—he wondered in confusion. Then it dawned on him. It must be related to the classy visitors who came to the spa late at night. They certainly didn't want prying eyes to see them in this place, naked and in questionable company, so heavy steam was the best cover. Okay, but where were they? Fair enough, they couldn't be seen, but they should be audible. The business they were here for wasn't exactly quiet. And yet there was still deep silence all around.

It must be that they had not have arrived yet.

All the better for him. He could be incognito somewhere, invisible and silent in this cloud, since he would be the only one not in someone's company. If he hadn't remembered the general layout of the bathroom, he would hardly have been able to find his way now. The swimming pool lay to the right, while the wooden loungers were lined up on the left. With any luck it was still like that.

This time he held out both hands in front of him and walked cautiously a little to the left. He encountered the first obstacle with his leg. His shin bumped lightly against a lounger. He removed the towel from his neck and, groping, spread it over the ribbed surface; he raised the top section a little, then stretched out on the lounger.

The minutes began to drag slowly by, and nothing was happening.

I was wrong, Fyodor Mikhailovich concluded after a while. I shouldn't have entered this gray nothingness. This is exactly what death might look like. It's best to get out of here while I can still remain unnoticed, before those who like this kind of atmosphere show up. It could happen at any moment, and if I'm discovered, I won't be able to avoid unpleasant explanations.

He started to rise from the lounger, but his movement was interrupted.

"Good evening." He heard from somewhere on his left the words in Russian that startled him. The elderly man's voice could have come from the adjacent lounger, but also from one further away. Without the help of his sense of sight, he was unable to judge the distance.

Several long moments passed before he replied, "Good evening," then added after a short pause, "How did you know I was Russian? You can't see me. And even if you could..."

"At this time of the year, there is hardly anyone else in Wiesbaden except Germans and Russians. A German would never enter a place like this unless someone checked his card and let him in."

"I left my hotel card at the reception desk. It's valid as an entrance ticket. I can't be blamed if there was no one on duty when the spa was still open."

"A German would wait for someone to show up. Disciplined people."

"And how did you get in? Though I don't know when you got here. Maybe there was someone to let you in then?"

"I arrived a little before you. There was no one then either."

"I feel better now. So, it's not only the Russians who are undisciplined. You speak Russian well, although with a slight foreign accent. I don't recognize it. It is neither German nor French."

"Indeed."

They fell into silence for a moment.

Fyodor Mikhailovich cleared his throat. "I'm going to leave now. I don't like being in this cloud. I didn't expect it. You don't mind?"

"I was bothered more by the horrible tobacco

smoke and the smell of sweaty gamblers in the casino."

"You've been to the casino?"

"Like you."

"How do you know I was there, too? If you saw me there, you still can't see me here. You don't know what I look like."

"I don't need to see you here. I can hear you, and I remember voices very well."

"I don't remember saying much in the casino tonight."

"You did. For some time you asked the croupier to place bets for you. I heard you well. I was standing at the same table, across from you."

Fyodor Mikhailovich thought a little. "No one caught my eye from the other side of the table. Maybe I would remember you if I saw you..."

"I doubt it. You were completely engrossed in the game. You didn't notice anything else. Especially near the end, when things went downhill..."

"My luck turned its back on me tonight..."

"It didn't seem like it."

"Rather?"

"Like you gave up on the game plan. That's where your discipline failed too. Also a typical Russian trait. And you did just fine as long as you stuck to the plan. At one point you had a nice stack of chips in front of you. But then it was as if the devil got into you..."

"You seem to have done nothing but watch me. Did you even play?"

"No. I didn't go to the casino to gamble."

"Why, then?"

"To watch the players. A veritable gallery of colorful characters. Like in a novel."

"You're a writer?" asked Fyodor Mikhailovich after a moment's hesitation.

"I'm not. And even if I were, I wouldn't write about gambling. There is nothing more to be written on that subject after your novel *The Gambler*."

"You know about me?"

"Of course. Why does that surprise you?"

"I don't expect to be recognized in the casino. Gamblers aren't usually fans of literature."

"Obviously there are exceptions."

"So you liked *The Gambler*?"

"A great novel. It should be required reading for anyone visiting a casino. To know what awaits him if he gets carried away and loses his head. It's a shame that tonight you didn't abide by the wisdom of your own work..."

"The devil got into me, as you said... It's quite a coincidence that I should meet one of my readers in such a place." Fyodor Mikhailovich mechanically made an arching motion with his hand through the cloud, forgetting that his conversationalist could not see him.

"A meeting like in *The Double*..."

"You've read *The Double* too?"

"I've read everything you've written."

"I am quite honored. I don't know anyone else outside of Russia who has read all my works." He paused for a moment. "This, admittedly, is not quite like in *The Double*. If you remember, the meeting there is not really accidental, although it seems to Golyadkin at first that it is..."

"This one isn't accidental either."

"What do you mean?"

"I knew you would come here. I left the casino a little before you so as to wait for you here."

"You had no way of knowing I would come here. I didn't know it myself. I decided to stop by at the last moment, when I was already in front of the entrance."

"It wasn't hard to guess where you were going. Could you have gone anywhere else without a penny in your pocket? Only the Turkish bath was free."

"I could have gone back to the hotel."

"Into a room without heating, with a candle stub that would go out in half an hour? If they gave you that much. German hoteliers are merciless towards guests who don't pay their bills."

"The news, I see, is spreading quickly," retorted Fyodor Mikhailovich after a short silence.

"Bad always faster than good. They won't report you to the police yet. It wouldn't be in their interest. They're still hoping that you'll somehow get the money you owe them, and you couldn't do that from a jail cell. In the meantime, they'll keep you as meagerly as they can."

"Don't worry, I'll get the money tomorrow. I will write to my wife. She will send it to me."

"She won't. Not even Fyodor Mikhailovich could

write such a miraculous letter. Anna Grigoryevna simply has nothing left to pawn."

Silence fell again upon the cloud of steam.

"Who are you?" Fyodor Mikhailovich finally broke it in a low voice. "Why did you wait for me here? What do you want from me?"

"I am someone who is very curious," came also the muffled reply from an indeterminate distance. "I want to know everything there is to know about you. Even more than that."

Fyodor Mikhailovich nodded his head for a few moments without saying a word, then heaved a loud sigh.

"The Third Section. I'm amazed, I must admit. I knew that our Imperial Secret Police were powerful, but not that they had spread their tentacles abroad this deeply. How did you manage to get hold of Anna's last letter? You could only find out from there that she had nothing left to pawn."

"It was not necessary to obtain Anna Grigoryevna's letter. Although that could also be done. German hoteliers are not as innocent as one imagines. For an appropriate tip, they would give up the key to your room while you are not in it. Even postal officials would not hesitate to hand over the letter to a generous interested party for a while, before delivering it to you. However, it was simpler to follow your wife. She went to the pawnshop in a winter coat and returned home without it. She was shivering with cold the whole way. It was really freezing in Dresden yesterday."

"So, you keep Anna Grigoryevna under surveillance! Why on earth?"

"No one knows you as well as your second wife."

"Of course she knows me well, but you still have nothing to learn from her. My political beliefs have long since ceased to be controversial. I have atoned for the delusions of my youth, I am no longer carried away by socialist ideas, I am a great supporter of tsarist rule. If not, would you allow me to travel abroad?"

"There's something else interesting about you besides your political beliefs."

"What else could the Third Section be interested in? I thought you were engaged in more serious business than the financial difficulties of Russian writers with a gambling habit."

"I certainly deal with more serious business than the Third Section. I am only mildly interested in your political beliefs by the way. And, just between you and me, I liked you better as a young socialist utopian than now as an inveterate tsarist. But you are much more interesting to me than all that precisely as a writer with a gambling habit who is up to his neck in financial difficulties."

Fyodor Mikhailovich squinted, straining to see through the white fog.

"I misunderstood you. You speak Russian well, but maybe you meant to say something else..."

"You wrongly assumed I work for the Imperial Secret Police. Besides, it isn't as powerful as it wants to make itself out to be. Especially not abroad.

They do have their man in Dresden, but he's a pretty useless guy. In any case, he is not at all interested in you or Anna Grigoryevna. At least on that head you can rest easy."

"How... do you know that...?"

"Because it's my job to know. If the Third Section knew what I know about you, they'd be a lot more interested."

"What do you know about me?"

"I know, for example, who all you met abroad. Here in Germany, in Switzerland, in London, in Prague... Among them were quite a few who are of considerable interest to the Third Section. Bakunin, for example, Herzen..."

"Those were all," interrupted Fyodor Mikhailovich, "unimportant meetings. Mostly random. Irrelevant topics were discussed. That is to say, things that would pass the Third Section by altogether."

"It wasn't always like that. Quite... sensitive... political issues were also discussed. Especially with Bakunin..."

"Even if it were so, and it is not, you can't know that. I always spoke with Bakunin in private. Without witnesses..."

"It just seemed that way to you. Every word you said was recorded. A quite valuable testimony."

"That's not possible. I don't believe you."

"Need I remind you how you replied when Bakunin asked how you viewed your revolutionary past?"

"You work for some foreign service, don't you?"

said Fyodor Mikhailovich after another hesitation. "It's clearly far more skilled than the Imperial Secret Police. But what do you want from me? If you're thinking of blackmailing me with what you know about me, I don't see what you're hoping to gain by it. I'm just a penniless writer with no ties to the Russian authorities. I am not privy to any important secrets that might interest you."

"I don't work for any service. Neither Russian nor foreign. If I did, I'd hardly be interested in your distant past. And I am enormously attracted by it."

"What distant past?"

"Your youth. Let's say, when, as an eighteen-year-old, in 1839, you were also left without a father, having lost your mother two years earlier."

"Why that time?"

From the thick steam came, instead of an answer, a question: "What do you know about your father's death?"

"About my father's death?" Fyodor Mikhailovich repeated in surprise. "What we were told. That he was killed by serfs. In Darovoe, where he lived after he retired."

"No one killed Mikhail Andreevich. He died of a cerebral hemorrhage on June 14, 1839."

"Where did you get that?"

"I saw the death certificate. It was even signed by two doctors, not just one. Cause of death: apoplexy."

"Where did you see the death certificate?"

"Where death certificates are kept—in the archives."

"I haven't heard of anyone else seeing it."

"Nobody was looking for it. It didn't seem to be of interest to anyone."

"I would certainly be interested, but I had no reason to doubt what we were told. At the time of my father's death, I was in Petersburg, with my brother Mikhail, at the Military Academy..."

"Your father had his first stroke precisely because of the Academy. The news about the troubles of the two of you during enrollment was hard for him. He was able to recover from that first one, but not from the second."

"Then where does the story come from that our father was killed by serfs?"

"It was invented by one of the neighbors who had his eye on your property. If they convicted the serfs of murder, your property would be left without laborers, so the neighbor could buy it for nothing. Fortunately, an investigation was conducted. It lasted more than a year. The serfs were eventually freed."

"And you found information about that in the archives too?"

"Partly in the archive and partly in another way."

"In another way?"

"Yes," replied the voice from the cloud, as if that explained everything, then changed the subject. "Do you know who among the Petrashevtsy worked for the Third Section? Who gave them regular reports on everything that happened at the meetings of your circle?"

Fyodor Mikhailovich unconsciously shrugged his shoulders.

"I thought about it for a long time in prison. It could have been any of us. Even Petrashevsky himself. To others, I was probably suspicious too..."

"Antonelli."

"Antonelli? Not possible! I mean, he seemed really stupid. It's like he lost his way among us. He never said anything. He just sat there with his mouth half open and his eyes dull, as if he didn't understand a single word."

"Just what a police informant should look like: inconspicuous, like someone you'd be the last to suspect. And he was actually a very bright guy with an excellent memory. His reports to Liprandi contained almost every word spoken at your Friday gatherings."

"I never would have thought..."

"To keep secret who the spy was, Antonelli was also sentenced to prison. Only ostensibly, of course. He was temporarily removed from Petersburg. He has made considerable progress in the service in the meantime. He no longer delivers reports. Now they deliver them to him. He was even decorated for exposing the Petrashevtsy."

"And you're not a Third Section man after all? Sly as Antonelli. How else would you know all this? The imperial police guard their secrets strictly."

"I have my own ways and means. Magical, one could say. They were especially useful to me on December 22, 1849."

A few moments passed before Fyodor Mikhailovich spoke again.

"Really? And how is that?"

"I found out what no one else did. Not even the Third Section, although they had their ears pricked up so that not a word escaped them. After they brought you before the firing squad, the priest approached you and held out the cross for you all to kiss one by one. Everyone did it silently—except you. When he was in front of you, you leaned towards him and whispered something in his ear for several long moments, until he flinched, stepped away from you—almost jumped—and hurriedly crossed himself three times. Hardly anyone noticed this little annoyance, but that's how it was, wasn't it?"

"It is."

"Do you want me to tell you what you told him?"

"You don't have to. I believe you know. But you didn't need anything magical for that. Damn priest, he deserved everything I told him then. And a hundred times worse. How much did he get to reveal to you what amounts to a sacred confession?"

"He got nothing. I didn't need to tempt him. And he could have kept the secret by lying to me. My magical way is more reliable though. But, how's your back?"

"My back?"

"Do your scars still sting sometimes?"

"What scars?"

"From the whipping. In the prison in Omsk."

"They didn't flog me in Omsk," quietly replied Fyodor Mikhailovich.

"They did. That description of the whipping from *House of the Dead*—that's autobiographical. A barrage of soldiers, encouraged by lieutenant Zherebyatnikov, broke even the most stubborn prisoners with whips. However, you held on heroically. You didn't cry out once, you just moaned. Amazing for someone not at all die-hard. And you could have avoided all that. If only you had let go of that rope..."

"Roznovsky's ax fell into the river. I still remember his name. He had to get it out, and he didn't know how to swim. He would have drowned if I hadn't pulled him out by the rope we tied under his arms. And just then, the drunk Krivtsov, the warden of the convict colony, came by..."

"Saving another, you almost paid with your head..."

"Almost, yes. For weeks I lay in the hospital between life and death. That's when I experienced my first epileptic seizure. And got an ugly nickname..."

"Corpse."

"My hat's off to you. You are really well informed. I was convinced that nickname had stayed behind in Omsk forever. I never told anyone about it. I'm ashamed of that whipping. How did you find out about my disgrace? Did you meet any of the guards who beat me, or any of the prisoners who were amused by the beating? Or again in some magical way of your own?"

"In a magical way. Your new novel, *The Eternal*

Husband, also contains autobiographical elements, doesn't it?" The disembodied voice waited a moment for an answer, but when there was none, it continued: "A very interesting topic. A husband who stays married, even though he knows his wife is cheating on him..."

"Ugly rumors!" Fyodor Mikhailovich's voice trembled with excitement. "Marya Dmitrievna did not cheat on me."

"You knew, of course, that she did not view marriage as sacred. She accepted your advances while her first husband was still alive..."

"That was something else. Alexander Ivanovich was aware that his end was near. Since he could not provide for his wife, he saw me as her saviour. He gave us his blessing..."

"Just like you gave yours to Vergunov. Love works wonders. You loved Marya Dmitrievna madly. So much so that you got over the fact that she spent the eve of your wedding with her handsome lover. And also when he moved to Semipalatinsk to be close to her, and then followed the two of you when you were finally allowed to return to Russia..."

"You cannot know with whom Marya Dmitrievna spent the night before the wedding," snapped Fyodor Mikhailovich. "Would the lovers let you into their room to hold a candle for them? No amount of magic could make that happen..."

"They didn't let me in. But I still stayed there for a while. Just to be certain what was to come. Then, of course, I prudently withdrew. I don't have voyeuristic tendencies."

"And for that short time I suppose you were hidden under the bed? Like in some cheap vaudeville."

"Don't be like that. Great writers also write about hiding under the bed. In one of your stories, you placed both a husband and a lover there at the same time. However, I didn't hide. There was no need for that. I was standing in the middle of the room."

"And the loving couple didn't mind that? Admittedly, it might have been dark. Marya Dmitrievna was very shy. The light was rarely on in our bedroom."

"They didn't put it out."

"Then there is no other possibility—you must have been invisible."

Fyodor Mikhailovich thought he heard a sigh come through the steam.

"There is no other possibility."

The silence persisted this time.

"I was also invisible," the voice finally continued, "on all the other occasions we mentioned. Yesterday I stood behind Anna Grigoryevna, while she was sitting at your desk in Dresden, and read over her shoulder the letter she wrote to you. I followed you and Bakunin at a short distance while you were walking in that Prague park and talking conspiratorially, convinced that no one could hear you. I was the only one at your father's bedside while he was dying of apoplexy in the dacha in Darovoe. I attended one of Antonelli's visits to Liprandi, when he gave him reports on the Petrashevtsy. I was quite close to you and the priest while you were whispering to him before the firing squad. I was next to you in the boat when you pulled Roznovsky out of the river, and then closely followed your suffering when you ran the gauntlet after returning to the penal colony. Well, that's my magical way. Very convenient and reliable in the work I do."

The voice fell silent for a moment after the long enumeration, then added:

"Even now I'm invisible. That's the reason this vapor is so dense. If it weren't there, you would hardly have agreed to talk to a voice that seems to come from nowhere."

"You don't have to hide anymore. Feel free to show yourself. I understand who you are."

"Really?"

"The devil has come to collect. My gambling madness has matured. If I were alone, I would bear it stoically. What comes next can't be more difficult than what I've already experienced. And I deserved everything that happened to me. But I dragged poor Anna and completely innocent little Lyubov into it. I won't be able to bear their downfall. There's only one way out from here."

"Suicide?"

"Suicide. I have no choice. Enjoy my demise. That's why you're here tonight, isn't it?"

"Not everything is so dark after all. If I were the devil, it would at least have an upside. You would finally get an answer to the most difficult question that has been haunting you all your life. If there is a devil, there must be a God. They cannot exist without each other. They are inseparable."

"What good is that answer now? I just let God down by doubting his existence my whole life. No, I mustn't hope for his mercy. There is no salvation for me."

"There is. First of all, I'm not the devil. I'm not here to enjoy your pain."

"How come you aren't? So who else can be invisible?"

"God, for example."

Fyodor Mikhailovich coughed. It was some while before he caught his breath. Then he half-raised his hand to make the sign of the cross, but gave up in confusion.

"Don't get upset," came out of the invisibility as the echoes of coughing died away. "I'm even less God than I am the devil."

"So who are you, then?"

"Someone quite ordinary. Your biographer."

The silence was disturbed for a few moments only by the barely audible dripping that came from somewhere in the indeterminate distance.

"You expect me to believe that I have a very ordinary invisible biographer?"

"It's not easy to believe, I agree. But maybe you'll believe your own eyes."

As if disabled by snow blindness from seeing anything in the cloud, Fyodor Mikhailovich did not immediately understand what was happening. There was no movement or sound. Only when the outlines of surrounding objects began to appear did he realize that the vapor was quickly dissipating. It thinned as if the air itself had absorbed it. In no time, it completely disappeared without leaving behind any trace. Around him, views opened up on all sides of a large, well-lit room with a swimming pool.

For a while he just stared confusedly in front of him; then he stirred as if out of a deep meditation and began to look around frantically in disbelief.

"Where are you? Show yourself!"

"I'm right where I was," he heard a voice two or three steps to his left. "On the lounger next to yours."

Fyodor Mikhailovich quickly straightened up into a sitting position and stared at the empty adjacent lounger. In an instant, he was overcome by the urge to jump up and run away, but he couldn't even move, like being chased in a dream and freezing all of a sudden. Is that what's happening?—he asked himself. I'm just dreaming all this? However, he did not wake up, as usually happens after this realization.

"All of this so far," continued the biographer, "should have been more gradual and lasted longer, so that you would have had the opportunity to understand better what I am communicating to you. But unfortunately we don't have time. You're going to have an epileptic fit soon, and when you do, I won't be here anymore."

"How do you know I'm going to have a seizure?"

Fyodor Mikhailovich asked hesitantly. Addressing the void filled him with an uneasiness he had never experienced before. "No one knows the future."

"I know the past."

"I beg your pardon?"

"If you have been able to accept invisibility, I hope you can this too, so suddenly, without preamble. I'm from the future. For me, everything about you is—in the past. That's how I know about the impending epileptic attack."

"From which... future?" Fyodor Mikhailovich wasn't sure if he had said the question or just thought it.

"From a very, very distant future. By the standards of the nineteenth century, but also of many subsequent ones, it is an age of miracles. You have just experienced two yourself. There are many others."

"It's... it's... more than a miracle... pure fantasy..."

"It's not even fantasy in your day and age. Another thirty years were to pass before the first ideas about invisibility and time travel appeared in the works of an English writer."

A mischievous smile crossed Fyodor Mikhailovich's face. "What would Vissarion Grigoryevich say to this...?"

"Belinsky, yes. What did he say about your *The Double*? 'The fantastic can have a place only in madhouses, but not in literature, being the business of doctors, not poets.' It affected you permanently..."

"It has just stopped affecting me..." He fell silent for a moment, then made a vague gesture with his hand towards the adjacent lounger. "Is this necessary? It's not easy to talk to air. It's like I'm in Belinsky's madhouse where I fantasize talking to myself. Why don't you show yourself?"

"That would change the past. And the past is sacred. It must remain exactly as it originally occurred. There is no place for me in that original and unique past. I can only, like an invisible spirit, observe, record, study it..."

"But we're talking right now. Isn't that changing the past?"

"These are very special circumstances. There is no fear that our conversation will change the past."

"How so?"

"No one else has heard us, and you will have no memory of it. An epileptic fit will wipe it out. You won't even know how you arrived at the Turkish bath, let alone what happened here."

"I never have a good memory of what was going on before an attack, but it has never quite gone away completely."

"This time there won't be a trace. I know that for sure. I've seen your whole future. There is not even the slightest mention of our meeting in it."

"If I'm going to forget everything, why don't you let me see you as well as hear you?"

"There is another reason why it is impossible, no less important than the first."

Fyodor Mikhailovich waited a while for the biographer to say something more, but as there was no continuation, he asked, "So, you've seen my future too?"

"I have. Both past and future. Your whole life."

There was a brief hesitation. "Can you tell me something about the future? Or is that also impossible?"

"It's only possible because you'll forget everything. Otherwise I would never tell you. Among other things, because I would ruin the rest of your life. You can't go on living if you know what's going to happen. Even if only the best is ahead of you. Everything becomes terrifyingly predestined. There is no longer the main bedrock of life—free will..."

"I wrote about it. Those are my words, aren't they?"

"Yours, yes. So, do you want me to reveal to you what awaits you, or perhaps you don't want to know anything about it even for a short time?"

"You're sure I'll forget?"

"Totally."

"Let me hear, then..." almost whispered Fyodor Mikhailovich.

"You will have two more children—two sons. Fyodor and Aleksey. Alyosha will not even live to be three years old. He will die from an epileptic fit..."

"Oh, God..." Fyodor Mikhailovich clutched his head. "I shouldn't have..."

"You will write three more great novels: *Demons*, which you are just starting, *A Raw Youth* and, near the end of your life, *The Brothers Karamazov*."

"Karamazov? An unusual family name. Black

people... Could you tell me something about that last book? Quite succinctly, in a few sentences."

"How could I condense nearly a thousand pages of that masterpiece into a few sentences? It would be barbaric, blasphemous..."

"Of course, of course... I just thought... Curiosity, you know... I'm sorry..."

"You will publish the magazine, 'Diary of a Writer'. It will contain only your writings. You will become famous throughout Russia with your speech about Pushkin on the occasion of the unveiling of his monument."

"About Pushkin..." A smile spread across Fyodor Mikhailovich's face for a moment.

"Your financial situation will improve as Anna Grigoryevna convinces you to start publishing your own works. However, you will never become wealthy. By the way, you will stop gambling. Tonight was the last time you played roulette."

"Really?"

"Yes. Unfortunately, your health will only deteriorate. That's a real shame. What else might you have written but for that? Alas, you were born too early. Only a century and a half later, all the ailments that tormented you will be treated quickly and easily."

"What do I die of?"

"From an aneurysm, January 28, 1881. A blood vessel in your lung burst. In those days it was not possible to stop the bleeding. You didn't suffer much. You passed away in the evening in your bed, surrounded by your family."

"That's good. I've always been terrified of the possibility of dying alone in a foreign land..."

"You had a huge funeral. Many thousands of people saw you off. Your grave is in the St. Alexander Nevsky Lavra in Petersburg."

"How strange," said Fyodor Mikhailovich after a moment's thought. "You know a lot more about my life than I do..."

"What kind of biographer would I be if I didn't know your life through and through? I know what you've been doing literally every day for sixty years. You must have forgotten some of it, but I remembered everything, noted it down. Don't worry, everything is saved, every little detail."

"Well then, you have devoted almost your entire life to me. I am quite honored."

"It has been a great honor to deal with you."

"That means I'm not yet forgotten in that distant time of yours... the time of miracles?"

"Forgotten? How could you be forgotten? There were great writers after you, of course, but you are still one of the greatest. And your biography is truly incomparable. All the things that happened to you in only six decades..."

"Yes, it's not a very old age. If I had lived a little longer, maybe I really could have written more books... important books."

"The second part of *The Brothers Karamazov*, for example. You announced it in the preface to the first one."

"Really? I was optimistic. Nothing will come of it."

"Maybe it will."

"How? You have seen my future. There's no second part, is there?"

"There isn't, but there will be a future sequel, so maybe there will be."

"I do not understand you."

"It's not easy to understand, I know. Something else from the treasury of the time of miracles. More fantastic than all the previous ones. You will die at the end of January 1881. That is unchangeable. I was at your funeral, after all. But you will be revived."

Fyodor Mikhailovich squinted at the empty lounger he was talking to.

"Resurrection?"

"What you've been hoping for all your life. Without which it seems to you that life has no meaning..."

"But it doesn't work like that... I mean, even the greatest human miracles aren't enough..."

"They are, though. We've already worked them."

"You resurrected someone?"

"Many great writers, the very cream of world literature. You will find yourself in excellent company. They can't wait for you to join them. Your arrival has been announced to them."

Fyodor Mikhailovich began to shake his head. He wanted to say something, but he couldn't find the right words.

"How do you imagine what follows resurrection—eternal life?" the biographer continued.

"I don't know... Who could imagine that...?"

"This is how it looks there. Resurrection is just like waking up in the morning. It's as if you woke up the next morning after you died—and just kept on living. As if dying was only a bad dream. It will be you in every way. All aspects of your personality, everything that makes you a unique human being, will be there."

"Entelechy?"

"Entelechy. Some things will be even better than before. Your memory, for example. You will remember your entire past perfectly."

"I'm already beginning to forget, even my own books, and that's terrible..."

"A shock awaits you that morning too. A pleasant one. When you look in the mirror. Instead of a decrepit old man, with traces of various diseases, you will see a thirty-year-old fellow in full strength, with lush hair and toned skin. And that will not change. You will remain at that age forever. There is no aging in eternal life."

"When will I be resurrected?" There was a hint of impatience in Fyodor Mikhailovich's voice. "The morning of January 29, 1881?"

"That is not possible and would not make sense. You will come to life in the time of miracles that is the only right setting for your return."

"And where will it be?"

"On the Island of Writers."

"The island of...?"

"In your own house, on an island inhabited by

great writers from earlier times. Everything is arranged there to make it as convenient as possible for you. You don't need to worry about anything, you don't have any obligations, nothing bothers you. You can write to your heart's content if you want... Or do anything else."

"Heaven..."

"Better than anyone ever imagined."

"Only writers are resurrected?"

"Not only them. Other artists also have their islands. It is a whole archipelago of art. You will meet them all. Everyone is looking forward to your arrival."

"What about the other people?"

There was no immediate response from the empty lounger. "I owe you an explanation," the biographer finally said. "I told you there was another reason you couldn't see me, remember?"

"I remember."

"It's not just that my physical appearance here would change the past, regardless of whether anyone would see me or not. I cannot appear physically because I have no physical appearance at all."

"Everyone has a physical appearance," replied Fyodor Mikhailovich after a short silence. "There are no ghosts..."

"I'm not a ghost."

"So what are you then?"

"Artificial intelligence, but don't even try to understand what that means. Everything will be explained to you step by step on the Island of Writers."

"And... natural... intelligence? People? What about them?"

"The natural ones are no more. They did themselves in. Only we, the artificial ones, are left to save what can be saved. Firstly, that which is most valuable. Art. But let's leave it at that. We don't have time. Your seizure will begin at any moment."

"If I'm left here alone, there will be no one to help me."

"There's the spa staff. They are back in their places. And when you come to, you will find some money in your coat pocket. Just enough to pay for the hotel, purchase a train ticket, and buy back Anna Grigoryevna's winter coat once you get to Dresden."

"Where did that money come from? I gambled it all away..."

"What happened to you in the casino will also disappear into oblivion. You will convince yourself that you didn't completely lose your head at roulette. After all, how else could it be?"

"And if I do come into temptation..."

"Don't worry, you won't. I told you the gambling is over. Trust your biographer."

All that was left was to say farewell, but Fyodor Mikhailovich couldn't think of anything suitable. "See you soon" made no sense because he hadn't seen his interlocutor at all, and "goodbye" could mean that he didn't believe what he had heard from him. While he was hesitating, the biographer spoke again.

"One more thing to finish with. You may have

wondered why I chose this particular day for our meeting. There was another reason besides your impending oblivion. Tonight was the closest you've ever come to suicide. It had to be prevented. It would be a real disaster if, because of your fleeting despondency, we were left without what you have yet to write."

But if it had to be prevented, then that meant... However, there was no opportunity for Fyodor Mikhailovich to complete the thought. From the deepest part of his head came an orgasmic flash that consumed everything else. The light was not empty as usual. A sight blossomed from its core. A sunny, sandy seashore, and on it, he knew somehow, a multitude of writers. Everyone was looking at him, smiling, waving at him. He also smiled, waved at them, and only a moment later everything collapsed into darkness, silence, and pain.

Into oblivion.

Acknowledgment

For some time I have been waiting for the right moment to express my immense gratitude to dear, dear Tamar Yellin, who has been invisibly present in all my books published in the English language. There may be more books after this one, but since I can't be sure of that, I must take this opportunity as if it were the last.

For a writer who writes in a minor language such as Serbian, and has the vain ambition to be known all over the world, it is of crucial importance how high the quality of his translations is, especially into English. Not only because this is the lingua franca of our time, enabling his works to be read by foreign publishers all over the planet, but also because they will often be translated from English, since many publishers will not be able to find translators from the original Serbian.

I have been lucky enough to have my books translated into English by very good translators: Mary Popović, Alice Copple-Tošić, Vuk Tošić and Randall A. Major. Even the best translators, however, need some help to make their very good translations even better. Not all of them, though, look favorably on this kind of improvement.

While I have been lucky with my translators, with Tamar it was as if I received a premium. She is simply a linguistic wizard who magically turns good translations not only into better ones, but into perfect ones—into a text that the reader is convinced is not a translation at all, but was originally written in English.

This applies to all my books, and especially to the novel *The Book*. This was the only time I made a mistake and allowed a work of mine to be translated into English by someone whose native language was not English. The resulting translation was completely unusable, until Tamar set to work to improve it—and performed a miracle. It turned out to be the best of all the English translations of my books, which is the more incredible when you consider that it is linguistically the most complex of my works, with lots of puns and various kinds of humor.

Today, I deeply regret that I was "diplomatically" considerate of other people's vanities, and so did not credit Tamar's contribution in every book. I can only hope that with this belated statement of my deepest gratitude for all she has done for me I have atoned for my lapse at least a little...

Zoran Živković

Contributors

About the Author

Zoran Živković was born in Belgrade, Serbia, on October 5, 1948. Until his retirement in 2017, he was a full professor at the Faculty of Philology, the University of Belgrade, teaching creative writing.

He is one of the most translated contemporary Serbian writers: by the end of 2023 there were 130 foreign editions of his books of fiction, published in 26 countries, in 22 languages.

Živković has won several literary awards for his fiction. In 1994 his novel *The Fourth Circle* won the Miloš Crnjanski award. In 2003, Živković's mosaic novel *The Library* won a World Fantasy Award for Best Novella. In 2007 his novel *The Bridge* won the Isidora Sekulić award. Živković has received two awards for his lifetime achievement in literature: The Stefan Mitrov Ljubiša (2007) and Ramonda Serbica (2023).

Živković is the author of 24 books of fiction:

The Fourth Circle (1993)
Time Gifts (1997)
The Writer (1998)
The Book (1999)
Impossible Encounters (2000)
Seven Touches of Music (2001)
The Library (2002)
Steps through the Mist (2003)
Hidden Camera (2003)
Compartments (2004)
Four Stories till the End (2004)
Twelve Collections (2005)
The Bridge (2006)
Miss Tamara, the Reader (2006),
Amarcord (2007)
The Last Book (2007)
Escher's Loops (2008)
The Ghostwriter (2009)
The Five Wonders of the Danube (2011)
The Grand Manuscript (2012)
The Compendium of the Dead (2015)
The Image Interpreter (2016)
The White Room (2022)
The Four Deaths and One Resurrection of Fyodor Mikhailovich (2023)

About the Artist

Youchan Ito was born 1968 in Aichi prefecture, Japan. She launched her career as a graphic designer in 1988, becoming a freelancer illustrator in 1991 and founding Togoru Co., Ltd. with her husband in 2000. In 2017 the company was reborn as Togoru Art Works. She works with a wide range of genres including cover art and design for science fiction, mysteries and horror titles, as well as illustrations for children's books.

www.youchan.com

www.ingramcontent.com/pod-product-compliance
Ingram Content Group UK Ltd.
Pitfield, Milton Keynes, MK11 3LW, UK
UKHW041843200726
13854UKWH00005BA/2035